Adapted by Meredith Rusu

©LEVEL-5/YWP. Produced by Scholastic Inc. under license from LEVEL-5.

Published by Scholastic Inc., *Publishers since 1920.* SCHOLASTIC and associated logos are trademarks and/or registered trademarks of Scholastic Inc.

ISBN 978-1-338-05444-6

10 9 8 7 6 5 4 3 2 1   16 17 18 19 20

Printed in the U.S.A.   40

First printing 2016

SCHOLASTIC INC.

It was a hot summer day, and fifth-grader Nate Adams was on a mission.

He needed to catch the biggest, most impressive bug ever. He wanted to prove to his friends that he was more than just average.

Nate swung his net over a rare beetle. "Gotcha!" he cried. "Yes! My friends will be so surprised when they see this!"

But little did Nate know, he was the one who was in for a surprise that day—his life would never be the same.

Nate raced back to his friends. "Bear, Eddie!" he called. "Check it out. I caught a rare stag beetle!"

Bear chuckled. "'Rare' must mean 'puny.'" He held out an even *bigger* beetle.

"No way!" Nate gasped.

Just then, the boys' friend Katie ran over.
"Hey guys! What did you catch?"

"Uh, I caught a stag beetle." Nate held out his
bug. He was hoping Katie would be impressed.

"Wow, Nate!" Katie said. She smiled. "It's just
like you. It's so . . . average!"

Nate couldn't believe it. Katie thought he was just *average*! Now he *really* needed to find the coolest bug ever!

So Nate headed deep into the forest. He chased after a golden beetle until . . .

"Where am I?" Nate wondered. He had stumbled into a clearing with an enormous tree at the center. Nate had never been in this part of the forest. In fact, he had a feeling no one had been here for a very long time.

That's when Nate noticed something strange. In front of the tree was a . . . capsule machine? It looked like something you might see outside a supermarket, but much older.

"What's that doing here?" Nate asked.

A voice started calling out to him. "Feed me, feed me," it repeated.

Nate hesitated. Then he pulled a coin from his pocket and inserted it into the slot.

A capsule tumbled out. Nate picked it up, opened it, and then . . .

WHOOSH!

Something magical and mysterious began whirling in the sky!

The wind swirled around Nate. An eerie voice cackled from the shadows. And then . . .

A strange being appeared!

"What's up, my friend?" the being said. "I am Whisper, at your service."

Nate was in shock. "You're a . . . a . . ."

"A ghost?" Whisper said. "Actually, I am a
Yo-kai—a mysterious being who makes strange
things happen in humans' daily lives!"

"But what were you doing in the capsule machine?" Nate asked.

"I was trapped in there 190 years ago by some self-righteous monks who said I was a menace to society," Whisper explained.

Nate blinked. "They had capsule machines back then?"

"Never mind the details," Whisper huffed. "What is important is that you have set me free! I am forever in your debt!"

"Uh, no offense, but I was just looking for some weird bugs," Nate said. "Not a weird . . . whatever you are. I want my money back!"

"I'm a Yo-kai!" cried Whisper. "I don't think you understand. You are a lucky boy! I happen to be a butler Yo-kai. I can solve your problems! If you want bugs, I can make that happen!"

Whisper began to do a wiggly dance. "Come out, little glow bugs. Time to light it up!"

Instantly, a cool glow bug flew past Nate.

But Whisper went too far. He summoned all the glow bugs in the forest! They swarmed on top of Nate in a big, glowing pile.

"No need to thank me," Whisper said.

"What have I gotten myself into?" Nate groaned.

Nate managed to dig himself out of the pile. But when he headed home, Whisper followed him. No matter how much Nate begged, the Yo-kai just wouldn't go away.

"Listen," Nate explained. "My parents won't let me have a pet, so . . ."

"Pet?!" Whisper cried. "I am no pet! I told you, I am a Yo-kai! An incredibly powerful spirit! Relax, I am invisible to everybody but you."

Just then, Nate opened the front door to his house. But something was wrong. He could hear voices arguing in the kitchen.

It was Nate's parents. They were fighting!

"How could you eat my last organic yogurt!" Nate's mom yelled at his father.

"It's not my fault that stuff is so delicious!" his father argued back.

"I can't believe it," Nate said. "They're fighting over yogurt. Who fights over yogurt?"

"Ah, yes," replied Whisper. "It's just as I suspected. It's because of *her*."

"Her?" Nate looked around the kitchen. "I don't see anyone else in here."

"That's because it's a *Yo-kai*," said Whisper.
"In order to see her, you need this!" Whisper
held out a funny-looking wristband. "This is the
Yo-kai Watch. Go ahead. Put it on."

Nate carefully put on the watch and pointed it at his parents. He pressed the button on the side. The watch lit up! An eerie beam shone into the kitchen.

Nate gasped.

In the glow of the watch, Nate could see a
huge purple blob behind his parents.
"Whoa! What is that thing?" he cried.

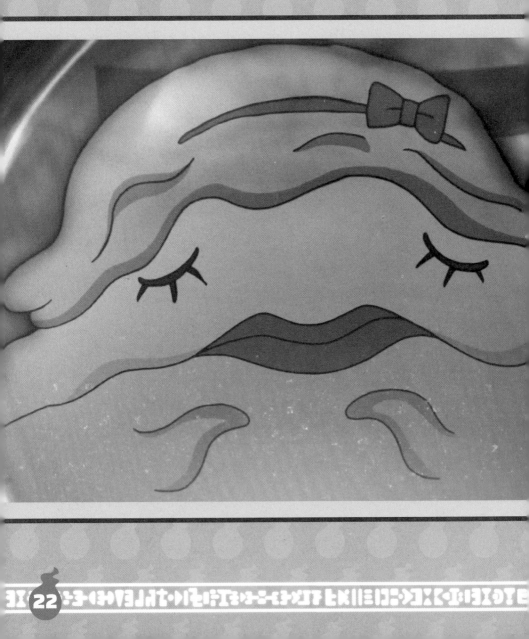

"That is Dismarelda," explained Whisper.
"She causes discord wherever she goes. This is
a very common event for Yo-kai to create. We
call it 'fighting about nothing.' Worst case, your
parents will continue fighting forever."

"What!" cried Nate. "I don't want that! How can we get her to leave?"

"The only way to stop a Yo-kai," said Whisper, "is by negotiation or confrontation."

"Fine, so go talk to her," Nate said. "You're the Yo-kai expert."

"Consider it done," replied Whisper.

He floated up to Dismarelda. "Hi there," he said cheerfully. "Would you mind getting your big blobby bottom out of here?"

That made Dismarelda even gloomier!

"You're making it worse!" cried Nate. He approached Dismarelda. "Please," he began. "My parents are pretty happy people. Could you leave them alone?"

Dismarelda groaned. "I'm sorry to be a downer. I had a fight with my husband and stormed off. No filter."

"Yo-kai have silly fights, too?" Nate asked. That gave him an idea. "My parents fight sometimes, but they still love each other. I'm sure you could make up with your husband if you just talk it out."

Dismarelda looked down. "Even if I wanted to, I don't know where he is."

"Look who I found!" Whisper suddenly called. A cloudlike yellow Yo-kai with a BIG smile followed Whisper into the kitchen.

"Dis!" the Yo-kai cried. "There you are! I'm so sorry we had a fight!"

"Meet Happierre," said Whisper, "a Yo-kai who brings happiness. Dismarelda and Happierre cancel each other out, creating normalcy."

Nate couldn't believe it. With Happierre and Dismarelda back together, his parents stopped fighting! Everything was back to . . . well, normal!

Later that night, Nate sat in bed. "So, Yo-kai really *do* exist," he said.

"Afraid so," said Whisper. "The only way to see us is with the Yo-kai Watch—which you now have!"

"This is crazy!" said Nate.

"Don't worry," Whisper insisted. "As long as I'm here, I will guide you and protect you from trouble!"

"Oh, and I should mention . . . that watch is impossible to take off. Whatever happens now, your life will never be the same!" said Whisper.

Nate gulped. It looked like he was in for an adventure . . . whether he wanted it or not!